PIG

gets the

Black

Death
(nearly)

Barbara Catchpole

Illustrated by metaphrog

Ransom

Say 'Hello'

to Peter Ian Green

- 'PIG' for short.

There are six PIG books so far. It's best to

read them in this order:

1. **Pig** and the **Talking Poo**
2. **Pig** and the **Fancy Pants**
3. **Pig** and the **Long Fart**
4. **Pig** plays **Cupid**
5. **Pig** gets the **Black Death** (nearly)
6. **Pig** Saves the **Day**

PIG gets the Black Death (nearly)
by Barbara Catchpole
Illustrated by metaphrog

Published by Ransom Publishing Ltd.
Unit 7, Brocklands Farm, West Meon, Hampshire
GU32 1JN, UK
www.ransom.co.uk

ISBN   978 184167 522 0
First published in 2012
Reprinted 2013, 2014, 2015

Copyright © 2012 Ransom Publishing Ltd.
Illustrations copyright © 2012 metaphrog

Death and dirt

Dirt, muck, spills, slop! I love dirt and mess. Filth is brilliant! I love to put my wellies – plop! – into a pile of sucky muck.

I'll tell you a secret. Get closer – no, closer ... Not that close! (Phew! What have you been eating? Socks?)

Now, I'll have to whisper, or grown-ups will hear and know that I've told you the truth:

The dirtier you are, the longer you live.

Honest! It's true! Doctors know it, but they

don't tell you. Doctors are all hoping to live to a
hundred and take over the world.

So I am going to
stay filthy and mucky
all my life. No baths
for me! No showers
either. I'm not even
going to go out in the
rain.

Come to think of it, we haven't got a shower
anyway. Dad did put one in over the bath once.
It fell off the wall and nearly did Mum a serious
injury. She threw it at him when he came home
from the pub.

I've decided I'm going to die at the age of one hundred and one, covered in mud. If I can get smelly and mucky enough, I might live forever.

I'll just need to keep away from all the doddering, old, smelly doctors. There'll be gazillions of them by then, wandering about like zombies. It will work for you too. You just need to get down and dirty!

I can help you get started, too. That's a bit of mega good luck for you!

I'd forgotten where my writing notebook was. I'd gone and left it on our kitchen table. Of course, with my family around, it got all sorts of muck and mess over it. Look at it! It stinks. If you rub it on your face and sniff it in, you'll be well on the way to living to be a hundred! You know you want to.

Have a good sniff! No need to thank me.

My family news

Justin Bieber (we call him that) is now going out with my sister. He's so short, he can't see her face. Mum says, looking at Suki, that it's just as well. Mum says he must just like the bits he CAN see

– and then she laughs
her big, belly laugh.
Mum keeps asking him:

    'What's the weather

    like down there?'

Suki, my sister, says:

    'Leave him alone,

    Mum! I'm not

    bothered if he's

    short – he's fit!'

Actually, Justin Bieber CAN see Suki's face – if he
goes upstairs and looks out of the bedroom window.
Then their faces are about level.

Gran is going out with Santa. (I Know. Yuk! Gross!) Still, at least I should get some good presents this Christmas.

My mum's too old to go dating, let alone my Gran. All grown-ups should pack all that in once they pass thirty. They're too old and wrinkly by then!

Still it's kind of sweet, really. Gran and Santa

help each other with 'old people' stuff. They sat in the Kitchen and cut each other's toenails the other day. Mum went spare.

'Get your feet off my kitchen table – I've got to cook on that!'

Mum is back to her old self now. She made a salesperson cry on the phone yesterday. Bet he thought he was safe in India. Ha! No one is safe from Mum, not even on Pluto. Mum has space missiles in the shed.

My baby brother – Vampire Baby – is doing OK. Mum calls him The Vampire Baby because he sleeps all day and is awake all night.

He's onto solid food now. That's what

grown-ups call the runny brown muck babies
spit at you and sling all over the walls.

Here is some for you:

I think it's neat that it comes out of him the
same as it went in, colour and runniness and
everything, with the peas still in it. Mum sticks a
finger in his nappy sometimes. I'm glad that's
not my job.

He doesn't eat much anyway. Most of it goes on
Mum and the walls. He got Raj with a huge
dollop on Thursday. Right between his eyes!

Vampire Baby sort of waits until you get near

and then sneezes it out. He's a pretty good shot.

Mind you, he's had lots of practice. Ask Raj!

Harry the Hamster is still at large. That means

he's escaped. I drew a wanted poster and put

it up on our fridge.

WANTED

£1,000,000,000,000 REWARD

So far Harry's eaten a pack of orange jelly, my Maths homework (except for number 3a – I couldn't do that one – it was long multiplication) and the finger off my blue school glove (right one).

(Ha! Result! Now I can pick my nose while wearing gloves – which is something nobody else in my year can do. Thank you, Harry.)

OK. I think I'd better get on with the story. Your teacher will be asking you soon what this book you're reading is about. Then you'll have to say:

'I dunno, I haven't got that far yet.'

So I'll tell you what to tell your teacher: this story is about dirt, injections, the Black Death and zits.

Now I'll tell it to you. Just as it happened.

It was all Raj's fault

Raj had come round to my house to use the loo. He does that a lot.

He doesn't get to use the loo very much at all at his house, because he's got seven sisters and he can't get into the bathroom. Hardly ever, anyway. He has to save it all up and do it round our house in one go.

His sister Tav had been in their bathroom for a record forty five minutes, twelve seconds. Raj timed her. He said it was to do with her eyebrows.

So after Raj had done whatever he needed to do in OUR bathroom, we walked to school.

Raj:

'Oh Pig, look! I've got a huge zit! I tried to squeeze it in your bathroom. What can I do to hide it?'

It WAS a huge zit. It was right on the tip of his nose. It was so huge it could have starred in its own film. It might as well have had its own ZIP code (or ZIT code, ha ha!).

The only thing I could think of that would help

would be for Raj to wear a paper bag over his head. I didn't tell him that, though. He had to get through the day.

I said:

> 'Perhaps it'll go down if you burst it a bit more. Try doing that at break.'

Raj:

> 'Perhaps I can do it in History. Sir gets very stressy during the starter – he won't notice. It's injections today, isn't it? First lesson. They said so in assembly.'

Me:

> '. . . . .'

I said nothing because I was terrified.

Injections

I hate injections. They stick a needle in you.

Then they push it in a bit further. Then they

squirt stuff into you.

Then they pull it out.

Then they say:

   'Don't make such a

   fuss!'

and

   'Look out – he's going!'

– just before you faint and hit your head on a

potted plant and get a huge purple bruise on

19

your face and soil in your hair.

I thought quickly. What would James Bond do? Obvious. He would miss registration.

If I missed registration, they wouldn't know I was in school. I could just join History in second lesson, and tell them I had been chased by a cow on the way to school, or had got caught in an earthquake or something.

One morning on the way to school Gary Blake had a swan land on his head. He was covered in feathers, all stuck on with swan poo. There's a lot of feathers on a swan. And a lot of poo inside it.

He looked like an explosion in a pillow factory.

Compared to that, getting chased by a cow wouldn't be at all bad. The teachers should be pleased with me for having such a small problem.

I told Raj not to say anything and I ran.

He said:

'But, Pig ...'

But I was already out of there.

So it was his bad. He should have run after me.

He didn't try hard enough to save me. It. Was.

All. His. Fault.

In hiding

I dodged into the changing rooms. Then I ran

smack into Dean Gosnall and Tiffany. I didn't

see what they were doing.

   'Sorry!'

I darted into the art room. I knocked over a large jam jar of purple paint. No time to stop! I made it into the English stockroom.

The bell went for first lesson just as I reached safety. Ha! They will never take James Bond alive!

I settled down for a snooze on a pile of 'Romeo and Juliet' books, halfway down. I was a bit tired. Vampire Baby had been shouting all night. Then he sleeps all day like a little red-haired angel. The rest of us wander round in the day looking like the zombies in that American programme I watch from behind the settee.

Suki wants to give Vampire Baby to another family.

Mum said:

    'Do we hate anyone that much?'

I think he should sleep in the garden shed. Or perhaps I could sleep round Raj's – although I might still be able to hear Vampire Baby from there. He's very loud. Perhaps we should swap homes. Raj could have a toilet AND a baby.

History

I snuck into the History class. I sat next to Raj.

Someone had thrown Sir's card searches out of the window in first lesson. They'd been in a strop after getting it wrong seven times.

We couldn't watch a video because the socket had chewing gum in it.

The room didn't have a whiteboard.

So Sir just had to talk to us. He told us about the Black Death. It was dead (joke!) interesting. Sir tends to bang on a bit. He really likes History. (Well he HAS been alive for most of it.) We help him out by shouting out a lot.

Sir said:

'It was back in the 1300s, before they had

electricity.'

'Please, Sir, how did they watch telly?'

'They didn't have televisions, Frankie. No
Wiis, Xboxes, PlayStations, iPads, iPhones or
anything else with a plug on it.'

'Well, Frankie, I suppose they talked to
each other. Yes, I expect it was boring.
Kylie! Use a tissue! They lit a candle when it
got dark.'

'My mum got a dead good candle in the
Next sale, Sir! It makes my brother
sneeze though. She says she likes the candle

more than she likes him, so she's keeping it. She says he can go, if he likes. I might get his room! I hope he goes!'

'Yes, a candle sort of like the smelly one your mum got from Next, Jade.'

'My mum's got one that smells of tropical breezes, Sir!'

'No. I don't think candles in the Middle Ages smelled of tropical breezes, Lexie. Nothing smelled of tropical breezes seven hundred years ago.'

'Tropical breezes must have smelled of

tropical breezes, Sir! Stands to reason, Sir!'

'Well, yes, Charlene, tropical breezes smelled of tropical breezes. But no, there were no scented candles from Next.'

'Or TK Maxx, Sir? 'Cos there's a new one opening down the retail park. It's next to the shop that sells those cheap pants with rubbish elastic that my mum says is a disgrace because her pants fell down next to the frozen peas in Tescos.'

'No, nor TK Maxx, Dean. Put your hand up, Brittany! No, there were no scented candles from the cheapo shop on the High

Street, Brittany. No. Well that's why they called it the Dark Ages. There were no scented candles at all.'

Sir began to look all stressy. I bet he missed his card sort.

Anyway, he told us how rats had come off the ships. The rats had fleas and the fleas spread the Black Death.

I could see in my mind, the rats marching along. They each had a tiny rat-sized thought bubble above their head. They were thinking 'Death to humans'. They all looked a bit like Dean Gosnall in rat form.

I was looking right at Blake Tippett's nitty hair as Sir said about the fleas. OMG! Fleas came from nits!

'Please, Sir!'

I said,

'Blake's got nits! Will she give us the Black Death?'

31

Then we all had to wait because Blake started crying. Sir had to send her to the medical room. Then a friend had to go with her.

Then another girl started crying just in case she had nits, and she had to go out into the corridor. Then her friend had to go with her. The room was nearly empty!

Then we all started talking about whether the stinky shampoo was any good for getting rid of nits and whether you could get the Black Death from hamsters or just rats and whether cheap pants were worth it ...

Until Sir shouted at us. He was definitely in a stress now:

'Can I PLEASE get on?'

When a flea bit you, you got the Black Death. That was more or less it. You died in agony after about three days and they took you away on a carty thing.

Tiff and Gary were having a loud fight over Tiff's lipgloss. It smelled of strawberry, so Gary ate it.

Sir started to shout again. He was going very red now. I think I saw a bit of steam come out of his ears.

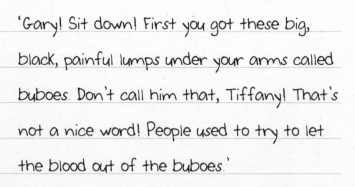

'Gary! Sit down! First you got these big, black, painful lumps under your arms called buboes. Don't call him that, Tiffany! That's not a nice word! People used to try to let the blood out of the buboes.'

Frankie had his hand up again. Frankie likes putting his hand up. It makes him feel clever. He hardly ever knows the answer and sometimes the teachers ignore him. He gets tired then and has to hold his arm up with his other arm.

'No, Frankie, I don't think Raj has got the Black Death. It's just a monster zit. It is unusually huge, though. No, don't all turn round to look at him!

'When the blood came out, it was black with green scum. Sometimes your nose, toes and fingers turned black.

'Hettie Greenburn, leave your arm alone! Well, it will hurt if you keep picking it. It'll probably turn septic and drop off! Oh, don't cry ... not again! Do you want to go out into the corridor? Saffina – go with her ...

'Right, class! That's the story of the Black Death. That's why injections are important. They help keep you healthy. Tiffany, leave your arm alone – or you will die horribly!'

Panic!

What was I going to do? Apart from die horribly, I mean.

Suddenly I thought about Raj's zit. Maybe he did have the Black Death! Perhaps it was coming back to England ... Everybody around me seemed to have zits or nits (or both). That rhymes! 'Zits' and 'nits'. It would make a good poem.

I HAD to get that injection – now! Otherwise I was DEFINITELY going to die of the Black Death. I probably had it already. Only an injection could save me.

Sir said you got black lumps in your groin. I'm not sure where that is, but I think it might be near my bits. Black lumps near my bits! Supposing my bits fell off? Or went black? Or went black and then fell off?

I ran down to the medical room. There was a queue of big girls there, all in their PE kit, waiting for the injection.

The reception was full of flowers because we had just had an Open Evening. I sneaked in behind a load of flowers. It was the size of a small jungle.

I pushed in between a girl with rabbity teeth and one with a huge red and yellow zit on her nose. Another zit! It WAS the Black Death!
Huge Zit girl:

'What you doing here? How dare you! Get out!'

Bugs Bunny Teeth girl:

'You are the one pushing in! Get off to the back of the queue!'

Me:

'I would be grateful if you would let me stay, beautiful ladies!'

Huge Zit:

'Push off, Gingernut!'

Now, at that point I may have made a remark about her zit and the other girl's teeth.

Anyway, it turned nasty. They were very big girls and they started pushing me backwards and forwards between them.

Zit pushed me to Bugs. Bugs pushed me back to Zit. I was like a ball in a pinball machine. Ping! Ding! Ding! Bleep! Crash!

Then Zit pushed me really hard and Bugs didn't even try to catch me. I ended up in a huge load of flowers. I had flowers in my hair, twigs down my trousers and I was dripping with green water.

A hand fell on my shoulder. Slowly I turned round. Oh no! It was the headteacher.

'Peter Ian Green! Where have you been? You've not even registered! Half the school is looking for you! You will be in detention for the rest of your life! Possibly even longer!'

I imagined myself as a manky old skeleton, still sat in detention. My mum was wailing:

'Please give me the body back so I can give him a decent burial!'

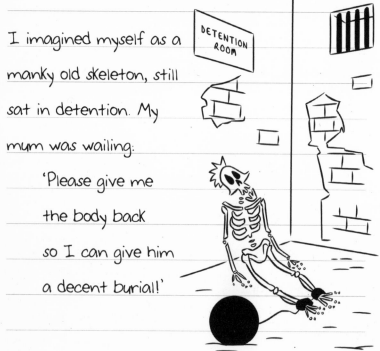

I've put the headteacher in bold because she was shouting a fair bit.

'Yes, but please, please, please, just let me have my injection first! It's a matter of life and death!'

The injection

'Girls! Girls! Girls!'

All the big girls in their PE kits turned and looked at me. I was covered in flowers and dripping wet. I had a pink rose in my hair and green water dribbling out of my nose.

The silence seemed to go on forever. I could feel their eyes on me.

'Why can't Pig have this injection, girls?'

(Headteacher still shouting.)

They all laughed at me. Every one of them. Some of them screamed with laughter!

'Because it's for girls, Miss! It's just for girls! It's not for boys! He thinks he's a girl, Miss!'

'Do you, Pig? Do you think you're a girl?'

The headteacher put her face right up to mine. She had a small zit on her chin. Probably not a BDZ (Black Death Zit) then, just a zit.

Divvy! Eejit! Moron! The insults hit my ears as the girls giggled and pointed.

Raj

Then the headteacher explained to me that I couldn't catch the Black Death from zits and nits. She was very kind.

After she stopped laughing.

And making a snorting noise.

And crying.

And saying:

    'Oh, it hurts!'

And after she'd started breathing again.

Raj said:

    'I knew the injection was just for girls. We

were told that in assembly when you were trying to play Angry Birds on your phone. I tried to tell you but you wouldn't listen. You never listen to me!'

Me:

'Sorry, did you say something?'
(No, I didn't say that really.)

I turned round and told him it was his bad, he had probably done it on purpose and I was never going to walk home with him again.

Raj said I was, like, in detention anyway, so he didn't care, so there. He was very upset. Dean Gosnall had said that Raj's zit was radioactive and glowed in the dark and it had made the girls laugh at him. It's true – his zit had grown during the day, until it looked like an alien that had landed on him.

On Monday, though, he waited for me in the library. He's a mate, Raj.

The good news

I had to tell Mum because she had to sign the detention letter. This was when she told me the great news.

She said:

'Thing is, Pig – think about it – you never get ill. It's because I never clean up.

'Your body has grown strong because you live with germs all around. I love cleaning. I do! Especially I like cleaning toilets.

'That's why everybody leaves it for me to do. Gran and Suki never do it! But it's OK. Cleaning the toilet is my favourite!

'I actually have to force myself not to do it, just to keep you well. It's science. You can't argue with science! I'm a modern mum!'

She wiped her finger under Vampire Baby's nose and dried it off on my notebook. Then she gave me a great sloppy kiss, before she sat down to watch 'Eastenders'. She was fast asleep in a second.

I saved you some of her drool.

So actually it's my mum that saved me from the Black Death. Not teachers or injections. My mum.

I hope your mum looks after you as well as mine does. Good health!

The next PIG book is

PIG
Saves the Day

About the author

Barbara Catchpole was a teacher for thirty years and enjoyed every minute. She has three sons of her own who were always perfectly behaved and never gave her a second of worry.

Barbara also tells lies.